WILD HOPE

WILD HEART MOUNTAIN: WILD RIDERS MC
BOOK TWO

SADIE KING

Why is forbidden love the sweetest?

When Kendra turns up at the Wild Riders MC compound looking for a job, I'm in agony.

I've been in love with my best friend's little sister since she waved us off for Iraq. I served with her brother. He's my best friend, my MC brother, and my business partner.

If I act on my feelings for his little sister, I'll not only dishonor my best friend, I'll be banished from the club.

But when a customer gets handsy with Kendra, my protective instincts kick in. I'll fight anyone and everyone to be with Kendra, whatever the price.

Wild Hope is a big brother's best friend, forbidden love, age gap romance featuring an ex-military mountain man and the curvy, innocent woman who claims his heart.

CONTENTS

1

TRAVIS

*T*he coffee burns my throat on the way down, and the bitterness sets my taste buds on edge.

I swallow the bitter brew and slide the cup back to Maggie.

"More cream."

"Sorry," she mumbles.

I try not to let her see me sigh. Maggie was only supposed to help out in the kitchen, but when a waitress quit last week, I convinced her to help out in the restaurant for a few shifts. The poor girl's as shy as a door mouse and as jumpy as one too.

"Don't worry about it." I give her a reassuring smile while making a mental note that we need to expedite finding new staff. "I'll cover the rest of the shift."

There're only two tables left, and we're not likely to get many drop-ins on a Monday afternoon.

Maggie gives me a grateful look and scurries out the back. She's a competent cook, but the woman doesn't know how to make coffee to save herself.

I skate around the back of the bar and tip out the sorry excuse for a brew. There's a sealed bag of Brazil's strongest coffee beans, and when I open it a rich aroma fills my nostrils. I breathe in deep and tip a bunch of beans into the grinder.

Wild Taste Bar and Restaurant is known for its craft beer, due to the brewery out back, but we also serve the best coffee on this side of the mountain.

With the beans freshly ground, I fill the porter filter and make myself the perfect cup.

A few minutes later, I'm back on my black metal barstool taking the first sip.

"Mmmm," I say to no one in particular. "That's good coffee."

While I wait for the caffeine to hit my bloodstream, I glance over the bar. Bike memorabilia adorns the walls with a vintage Harley taking pride of place. There're photos of the motorcycle club riding out for a charity event in our full Wild Riders MC leather jackets, and then the members dressed in their military uniforms for a Veterans Day parade.

The restaurant's unusual in that it's split in two.

The bar opens up to a dining area, and there's a VIP section over the road perched on the edge of the cliff face. The views from that side are stunning, looking over the valley below.

We've had to keep it closed the last few weeks due to staff shortages. It's hard to keep the service running on both sides when you're a waitress down.

I've been helping where I can, but on top of my regular workload, I'm exhausted.

As a founding member of the Wild Riders MC and manager of the Wild Taste Bar and Restaurant, there's a lot to do. The MC club owns the businesses, but Quentin and I run the place.

We've opened the brewery up for tours, and it's not going as smoothly as I'd like. The marketing has been too effective. Every tourist on both sides of the mountain wants a brewery tour, and we're booked up solid for the next several weeks. We're extending the tour times and hours, but so far there's no one to run them.

It's hard to get staff to stick around in the ass end of nowhere.

What attracted a bunch of ex-military bikers to a place is not the same as what most people want. After the military, I came here with my best friend Quentin and bike mad Raiden. It was the perfect spot to regroup, recover, and get our asses going on the next stage of life.

It was Raiden's idea to start the Wild Riders MC club, and he became president. Our compound comprises the group of businesses that have sprung up on the side of the mountain: the restaurant, the brewery, and the bike repair shop out back. We've got clubrooms at the back of the restaurant and rooms upstairs for whoever needs them.

The closest town, Wild, is a twenty minute ride away. And that's how we like it. Quiet, remote, and isolated. Perfect for a bunch of damaged soldiers.

But it turns out not everyone wants to live in the mountains. There are plenty of tourists to keep the bills paid, but finding staff who want to live in the middle of nowhere is a problem.

It's rare to get a quiet moment, and I sip my coffee and let my mind wander. As it so often does, I think about how good I have it up here: a thriving business, a cabin in the woods, my MC club with brothers who'd do anything for me. Yet, in still moments like these, there's a restlessness in my soul, a feeling like I'm missing something, like I got it all wrong.

I survey my restaurant. The table of tourists pouring over brochures, the couple finishing their lunch in the corner, the bikes parked out front, the noises from the kitchen as Chef preps for the evening trade, and the smell of hops from the brewery which permeates my clothes and is how I got my road name: Hops.

I should be happy, I should be content, yet there's something missing.

Like I've done so many times in moments like these, I pull out my wallet and slide the dog-eared photo out of the card holder. Me and Quentin stand upright in military uniforms. Between us is a woman with blonde hair falling over her shoulders. She's wearing shorts that show off thick creamy thighs and one leg is bent, her knee bending in towards the other, her heel in the air. Her smile is wide and lights up her sparkling eyes, which are the same deep green as the forest canopy.

I pulled this photo out so many times in Iraq that the paper is worn thin and there are spiderweb lines where it's creased around the edges. But Kendra's smile is as bright as it was the day the photo was taken six years ago.

Kendra was only eighteen when that photo was taken. Unaware of how her short shorts and throaty laugh made my entire body stir with desire. I suppressed it. She was an innocent girl and I was a man of twenty-nine, who had seen too much and was jaded by life. Besides, Kendra's my best friend's little sister. Off limits.

My parents moved to Australia once I left for the military, so Quentin invited me to spend Thanksgiving leave with his family.

Mrs. Harrison cooked a Thanksgiving feast, and we played board games. I spent the entire two weeks trying to keep my eyes off Kendra as she moved around the house, singing pop songs and dancing every chance she got.

That was before the accident that claimed her parents. Before her and Quentin's world fell into darkness.

Quentin left the army after his parents passed, and I soon followed. I visited my parents in Cairns, sweating like I was back in the desert. Then I followed Quentin to the cooler mountain.

By then Kendra was on the road, spending her inheritance and trying to outrun her grief.

Quentin used some of his inheritance for a down payment on the brewery, Raiden chipped in, and I used my military savings to stump up the other third, and the Wild Riders MC was born.

Life has been busy, life has been good, but I find myself pulling out the picture and studying Kendra's face more often than I like to admit.

"You haven't changed a bit."

I glance up at the throaty voice, and there she is. In the flesh. Kendra Harrison. All five foot two of her, blonde hair streaked with bright pink cascading over her shoulders, wearing knee-high leather boots and a skirt as short as the shorts in the photo.

My jaw hits the floor, and I want to grab my coat and cover her legs. No one sees those thighs but me.

Her smile is as broad as in the picture, but it doesn't quite reach her eyes. The cheeks are fuller, and she's lost the little girl look. Her figure has filled out; she's a woman now, with womanly curves a man could get lost in.

"Kendra." It's the dumbest thing to say, but I can't believe she's really here. "What are you doing here?"

She raises an eyebrow at me. "Good to see you too, Travis. Or should I call you Hops now?"

She's referring to my road name, which means she must have been in touch with Quentin. Son of a bitch never told me.

"Call me Travis." Damn, that sounds awkward. Like I've just met her, not like I spent Thanksgiving at her house and the last six years thinking about her.

Her eyes sparkle like she's enjoying my discomfort. "It's good to see you, Travis."

She dumps the duffle bag she's holding and strides over to where I'm sitting, the heels of her leather boots, clacking against the wooden floor and turning the heads of my customers.

I slide off the bar stool, still stunned by her presence when she wraps her arms around me.

Her hair smells like peppermint, and her perfume is musky. Her body is soft, and her feminine curves pressed against me cause my blood to heat. I hug her back, just as she pulls away.

Her arms loosen, and she kisses me on the cheek. Like a brother. She kisses me like a brother.

"There she is."

Quentin's deep voice rumbles across the bar, and I drop my arms guiltily as if he can see into my mind.

"Quentin." She squeals and runs at her brother. He sweeps her into his arms and twirls her around, making Kendra giggle. A jealous twinge rumbles through my heart. I want to make Kendra giggle like that.

"How did you get here?" Quentin asks. "I wasn't expecting you until tomorrow."

She holds her thumb out and Quentin frowns.

"You hitched?" We both say it at the same time.

Kendra rolls her eyes. "Geez, it's like having two over-protective big brothers. Yeah, I hitched from the closest town. Got a lift from a pregnant lady in a Caddy."

"Danni," I say, feeling relieved. Danni just married Vintage. Colter is his real name, but he goes by Vintage on account of his love for old bikes. It's not surprising he hooked up with a woman who drives an old Cadillac.

"Do you all know each other around here?"

"You're lucky Danni picked you up, but I don't want you hitching again." Quentin uses his stern big brother voice, but Kendra shakes her head at him.

"I don't think you can stop me, big brother."

Quentin turns a shade of purple, and I must look the same. There's no way I'm letting Kendra hitch a lift ever again. But before he can say anything else, Kendra puts her hand on his shoulder.

"Relax. I'm not going anywhere for a while anyway."

My heart skips a beat at her words. "You sticking around?"

"Didn't my brother tell you?" I look to Quentin, but he's got his eyes on his sister. He didn't tell me she was coming, and it makes me wonder if he knows how I feel about her. "He said you needed help, and here I am."

The thought of Kendra working here, working alongside me where I can see her every day, makes my stomach flip.

At that moment one of the prospects walks past,

and Quentin picks up Kendra's bag and hands it to him.

"Show Kendra to her room. She's taking the blue room upstairs until I can find her a place to stay. First shift's tonight. If you're up for it."

"Sure thing, big bro. Anything to help." She follows the prospect out of the room and I stare after her, trying to process what's going on.

Kendra is here, she's staying upstairs, and she'll be working in my restaurant for the foreseeable future. I'll get to spend every day with her, to watch her move, to talk and laugh with her.

"Can I count on you?"

I don't realize Quentin's been talking to me until he snaps his fingers. "Hey, Hops, where did you go?"

To an alternate universe where I wake up every morning next to your sister. But I don't say that.

"Sorry bro, just a lot on my plate."

"I'm on this work trip later in the week."

Quentin and the Prez are going on a road trip to visit some of our distributors and try to drum up more business. I'm staying behind this time to keep things running.

"I want you to keep an eye on Kendra for me. Help her settle in and make sure none of the guys get any ideas. I love my brothers, but if anyone lays a finger on my sister, they're out of the club."

He cracks his knuckles, and his face tells me he's serious.

"She's been through enough shit, and the last thing she needs is any grease monkey trying anything with her. I'll break the nose of any man who so much as asks her the time."

He slaps me on the back. "Can I count on you to keep an eye on her while I'm gone?"

I swallow hard, swallowing down the brief fantasy of anything I might have imagined for me and Kendra. Quentin's made it clear; she's off limits.

"Sure," I say, trying to smile. "You can count on me."

2

KENDRA

"Drinks for table nine."

The bartender moves two wine glasses out of the way to fit the last beer on the tray. I have to use two hands to pick it up and carry it over to the rowdy table in the corner. I take at least a minute to weave between the busy tables, stopping as a woman pushes her seat back right in front of me, nearly spilling the entire tray of drinks.

"Sorry, I didn't see you."

"No problem." I'm the queen of patience, having waitressed across the country for the last six years. It's all about smiling and waiting and keeping it together no matter what happens.

I set the drinks down at the table and collect the empty glasses.

Both the evening shifts I've worked have been

like this. I'm happy for my brother that the place is so busy. Business is good for him and the club.

I'm on my way back to the bar with the tray of glasses when Travis saunters in. My feet stumble, and water sloshes over the side of one glass. I catch myself before the entire tray goes down.

Damn, that man can still make me lose my balance.

I thought six years might have dulled my feelings, but when I saw him sitting at the bar this afternoon, his biker jacket on, a layer of messy stubble over his strong jaw, and silver flecked through his hair, my heartbeat went up several notches and it hasn't come back down. Now my palms are sweaty, and I'm having trouble concentrating on my tables.

I thought my girly crush on my brother's best friend might have dulled, but nope. It's turned from a girly crush to a womanly longing. One look at Travis's broad shoulders and tight white t-shirt and there's damp heat between my legs and my nipples are tingling.

Too bad he's not interested.

My hair falls across my face, and I curse myself for the pink streaks I've had for the last few years. I thought it looked edgy and cool, but to a man like Travis it probably shows how young I still am. His hair is peppered with silver, and there are crinkles at the sides of his eyes. He's the kind of man that needs a woman, not a too-chunky girl playing dress up.

"Excuse me. Can I get some ketchup?"

The woman's voice snaps me out of my thoughts, and I turn to her. "Sure." I give her my best smile. "I'll bring it right over."

I deposit the glasses at the bar and grab a bottle of ketchup to take back to the lady.

"Food's up for table eleven," the slight girl in the kitchen calls.

I give the lady her ketchup and head over to the serving hatch. As I walk past the bar, the skin on the back of my neck prickles. Glancing up, I catch Travis watching me. His dark eyes dart up from my butt, and he looks away.

Did I just catch him checking me out?

All kinds of heat courses through my body, and I wipe my palms on my apron as I get to the serving hatch.

"Someone can't take their eyes off you." Maggie waggles her eyebrows, and I glance back to see Travis staring at me again.

"He's been watching you all night," Maggie whispers. "Again."

Her mousy brown hair is pinned up under a chef's hat, showing off her round face dusted in freckles. I met Maggie when I arrived yesterday and liked her immediately. She's supposed to be a cook but has been helping anyway she can in the kitchen. She's quiet but observant and will be one hell of a chef one day.

I don't know where my brother found her, but she's so petite she looks like a kid working in the kitchen.

"I've known Travis for years," I say, trying to brush it off. "He's just being friendly."

"Un-huh," she says with a knowing smile.

The plates are slippery in my sweaty palms, and my feet seem to have trouble walking. I wish Travis would disappear into the back office so I could get on with waitressing without feeling like my knees are about to give way.

I deliver the food to table eleven. There are a bunch of empty glasses and I clear them off the table, holding the tray over my head and maneuvering through the crowded restaurant to get back to the bar.

Arlo, the bartender, is preparing a sampling board for table thirteen. They're a bunch of hipsters who must be staying at the ski lodge judging by the way they're dressed. They're the only ones here whose flannel shirts look freshly pressed and whose beards are neatly trimmed.

I shake my head to myself, marveling at what a

good thing my brother has going on here. The brewery provides decent beer for the locals and craft beer for visiting hipsters just like these.

I scoot around the side of the bar with my tray of glasses, thinking I'll put them in the dishwasher since Arlo is busy.

I don't notice Travis until I get around behind the bar. He's crouched down restocking the fridge. He stands up abruptly, and I run straight into the solid muscles of his chest. My feet stumble, my breath leaves my chest, and this time there's no saving the glasses.

The tray goes down. Glass shatters everywhere. The smashing sound silences the restaurant, and all heads turn to me.

There's a moment of utter silence. Then someone claps and the restaurant cheers, and everyone goes back to eating.

"I'm so sorry."

My cheeks heat with embarrassment. Of all the people to run into, it had to be Travis. I drop to the floor at the same time as he does, almost bumping heads. I pick up shards of glass, trying to ignore the fact that I'm so close to him I can smell his scent of hops and some musky male body wash.

"It's okay. I'll take it out of your pay."

I glance up at him, and his lips twitch. "I'm kidding. It happens all the time."

Now he's being nice. I've been waitressing for the last six years, and not once have I dropped an entire tray of glasses or seen anyone drop an entire tray of glasses. Travis must think I'm an incompetent klutz.

"I don't know what happened." I pile broken glass onto the tray while embarrassment claws at my skin. "I didn't expect you to be hiding behind the bar."

He chuckles, and it's a deep throaty rumble that I feel in my bones.

"I was stocking the fridge. I didn't mean to startle you."

He startled me the moment I walked in the door. I came back to help my brother and to see if my feelings for Travis had changed. That's a big nope.

Travis's hand shoots out and clasps me around the wrist. Heat from his touch skitters through my body, and my breath hitches.

"You've cut yourself."

I glance down at my hand, and there's a thin trickle of blood oozing from my index finger.

"Damn."

Travis lets go of my wrist, and I slip my finger between my lips. A metallic taste hits my tongue as I suck hard to stem the blood flow.

Travis makes a strangled noise, and I glance up at

him. He's staring at my mouth as I suck the finger between my lips.

His pupils dilate, and a low growl rumbles from his chest that I feel all the way to my core. My skin heats with embarrassment as I realize what this must look like, even as heat floods my panties at the hungry way he's looking at me.

Travis stands up quickly, and the moment passes.

"Get a bandage on that. I'll get this cleaned up."

He saunters out of the bar area without looking back.

I watch him go with a new lightness in my chest. Travis *is* attracted to me, I'm sure of it. If only I can get him to see me as something other than Quentin's little sister.

3

TRAVIS

*M*y palms are sweating, my blood is thundering in my ears, and my dick's as hard as the trunk of a pine tree in the forest.

It's bad enough that Kendra's been wiggling her curvy ass all night, her hips swaying as she weaves through the restaurant. I haven't been able to keep my eyes off her body. Then she goes and crashes right into me, her tits bouncing off my chest and the scent of flowers and perspiration trailing after her. But when she slipped her finger between her plump lips and sucked on it, I almost lost control.

An image of her full lips wrapped around my cock jumped into my head and I had to get out of there before I did something stupid, like throw her over the bar and claim her in front of the entire restaurant.

Because she's not mine to claim. She's Quentin's little sister, and there's no way she'll ever be mine. Not that she'd want an old man like me anyway. Kendra's a free spirit. She's been on the road ever since her parents died, moving from town to town doing work here and there.

Quentin's been worried sick about her, and so have I. Now that she's here, he'll do anything to make her stay. Which means I can't hit on her, even if I thought she wanted me. I can't fuck this up and have her leaving town. She's safe here, even if she can't be mine.

"Busy night out there?"

I jump at the sound of Quentin's voice, and he chuckles.

"What you so jumpy for?"

Because I'm this close to throwing your little sister over my shoulder and carrying her to my cabin.

I run my hand through my hair and try to hide what I'm really thinking.

"No reason, bro. Just a busy night."

He leans on the doorframe of the office, casting his face into shadow.

"You sure you'll be all right on your own with me and the Prez gone?"

Geez, I must be jumpy if he needs to ask that. "Yeah, I've got it under control. Especially with

Kendra here and Arlo helping at the bar. The restaurant is almost fully staffed."

"About Kendra…"

He takes a step into the office, and I tense. Has he read my thoughts, or am I just that obvious?

"Like I said the other day, I need you to watch her while I'm away."

My shoulders relax. He doesn't know the thoughts I've been having about her. He doesn't know that I'm the one who needs watching.

"I'll look out for her."

"Now that she's here, I want her to stay. I want her close so I can keep an eye on her."

The thought of Kendra living on the mountain, where I could see her every day, makes my heart sing. I won't have to pull out the photo. The real thing will be here.

"Make sure none of the guys try anything."

His voice goes serious, and he cracks his knuckles. "I don't want some asshole treating her bad and scaring her off."

The thought of another man with his hands on Kendra makes my fists clench.

"I'll make sure."

"Good. I'll kill any fucker who messes with her."

I nod. And he claps me on the shoulder, a grin returning to his face.

"Thanks, man. See you when we get back."

Quentin leaves the office, and I lean on the side of the desk. He wants me to watch his little sister, but he doesn't realize I'm the one he should be worried about.

4

KENDRA

*I*t's a few nights later, and only two tables remain in the restaurant.

One is a couple in the corner holding hands over the table. I'm trying not to feel envious of their easy laughter and the way they've spent the night talking and touching.

"That's Kobe and Hailey."

Arlo catches me watching them and leans against the bar next to me. There's a note of envy in his voice too. I guess I'm not the only one wishing I had a love like that.

"I served with Kobe. He's a good guy. They live on the other side of the mountain, near Hope. But we don't hold that against them."

The only other table is a group of hipsters that were on the brewery tour this afternoon. They've spent the entire evening since in the bar. What started as a sampling of craft beer led to downing pints like water and breaking into song.

"I've given them their last orders," Arlo tells me. "A taxi's on its way to take them back to the lodge."

"There's a taxi service around here?"

Arlo grins. "We've got a guy who comes up from Wild. He's not a registered taxi. Just uses his car occasionally to collect drunks like these."

I feel a tingle down my spine and look up to find Travis watching me. He's perched on a stool at the end of the bar with his laptop in front of him. There's a scowl on his face and Arlo must see it, because he pushes off the bar and away from me.

"Better get back to work," he mumbles.

Travis has been here all night, helping when needed but mostly tapping away on his keyboard while nursing a beer.

I've felt his eyes on me throughout the night, and every time I look up, I've caught him looking at me. He doesn't even bother to look away. He just keeps those intense eyes on me, his gaze following me around the room, making my blood heat and my core ache with longing.

There's no denying this attraction between us. No one looks at someone like that if they're not interested.

Every time I feel his eyes on me, my panties dampen and butterflies flutter behind my ribcage. Travis has had this butterfly effect on me ever since I was eighteen years old.

To think that he might like me back has my heart singing in all sorts of ways.

A cheer goes up from the corner where the drunk men are. One of them has spilled his beer on the table, and it drips onto the floor.

With a sigh, I grab a cloth and head over to the table.

"Sorrrry."

The man has red eyes and he's slurring. He lurches toward me as I approach the table, and his hand rests on my shoulder.

"What's your name?"

His breath stinks of beer and I dart forward, trying to get out of his grasp. But I'm not quick enough. His hand slides down my back, and his hand cups my backside.

I freeze at the contact. It's supposed to be a part of the job, being occasionally groped by drunk men, but I've never been able to get used to it.

The sound of a bar stool scrapes behind me, and a moment later Travis is grabbing the guy by the shoulder. The drunk man stumbles sideways, the grin slipping off his face.

"Don't fucking touch her."

There's a hard edge to Travis's voice that I've never heard before. He doesn't give the man time to apologize before he swings his fist. It connects with the drunk's nose, and blood spurts everywhere.

"What the fuck, man?" The man clutches his nose as blood drips into his hipster beard.

"Get the fuck out of my bar and don't come back."

Travis's face is red, a vein throbs in his neck, and his eyes glow dangerously. I've never seen him like this before. He's wild in this moment, my protector, and God help me, my panties dampen at the sight of him.

I get out of the way of the men, sure there's about to be a brawl and powerless to stop the male energy that's flying around the room.

Arlo comes out from behind the bar and Kobe joins him, standing behind Travis. They're a formidable sight. Three big, burly ex-military mountain men and two of them wearing bikers' patches.

The two groups of men face each other, sizing each other up.

I glance at Hailey and she's standing anxiously at the side of the bar, her hand on her pregnant belly. I go to her and take her hand, ready to flee through the back door if things get heated.

Luckily, there's one in the group of drunks who's sober enough to see sense.

"Come on."

He herds his friends to the door, and as soon as they're out of the restaurant the tension drops from the room.

"Are you okay?" Travis strides to where I'm standing with Hailey, the fire in his eyes still burning and making my knees weak.

I nod. "It was just a butt squeeze." I try to make light of it, but my words make Travis growl with anger.

"No one touches you." The possessiveness of his words make me shudder in a good way. But he's probably this protective of all his staff.

He lifts his hand to run it through his hair, and there's blood smeared across his knuckles.

"You're bleeding."

He winces as he flexes his fist. I don't know if it's his blood or the drunk man's.

"We need to get this disinfected. Where's the first aid kit?"

"My office."

I grab his wrist and lead him out the back and into the office. My heart's racing from the contact and what just went down. Travis stood up for me and took that asshole out.

I find the first aid kit and pull out a disinfectant wipe to mop up the blood. Then I get another one to clean out the cut.

"This might hurt."

I dab disinfectant on his cut, but he doesn't even wince.

"Tough guy, huh?"

Travis smiles. The fire has gone out of his eyes, and he's back to the affable guy I know.

"You can't be in the military and then cry over a minor cut."

It's not just a minor cut. The knuckles are turning purple, and they'll be bruised tomorrow.

"I'm gonna bandage this up for you. You need to rest it."

"Yes, doctor."

I glance at him, and he's smiling at me. My gaze darts to his lips, and I look down quickly before I do something stupid like kiss him.

"Why'd you leave the military anyway?"

I haven't seen Travis since he spent Thanksgiving with us six years ago. It was soon after that that my parents passed away and I hit the road. I heard from Quentin that he was back, but I could never bring myself to see him until now.

"My time was done, and I was needed back here." He gives me a funny look I can't interpret.

"Where have you been for the last six years anyway?"

It's my turn to be evasive. "Here, there, everywhere. The east mostly. Seasonal work in Kentucky and waiting tables in South Carolina."

Anywhere I could get away from the memory of my parents is what I don't add.

"What brought you back to the mountain?"

You, is what I want to say. It's been six damn years since I saw him, and he still plagues my dreams every night. No other man has ever lived up to Travis. I came back to see if I still felt the same, hoping that I wouldn't so I could move on with my life.

"To see if it felt like home yet."

He tilts his head. "You gonna stay?"

"That depends." I finish wrapping his hand and secure the bandage. Our heads are inches apart, and my heart's beating so loud he must hear it.

"On what?"

"If there's anything worth staying for."

There. I've said it in the most obvious way short of telling him I came back for him.

We stare at each other, our faces inches apart. I can't breathe.

Travis reaches his good hand up and cups my chin. He leans forward, and my lips part. I've been waiting for this kiss my whole damn life, and as he presses his lips to mine, all thought flies out the window. His lips are firm and warm and *hungry*.

His fingers grasp my neck, pulling me toward him and making my entire body light up. A moan escapes my lips. This is everything I ever dreamed of. Everything my schoolgirl self ever wanted.

The sound of the door to the restaurant swinging open has us jumping apart.

"You seen the mop?" Arlo asks as he swings his body around the office doorframe.

"Yeah." Travis's voice is tight with irritation. "In the cleaning cupboard."

"Not there, boss."

Travis sighs and heads for the door. He glances back at me, and his eyes are lit up like fire. "I'll be back in a minute."

He leaves the office with Arlo and I touch my lips, loving the way they tingle from his touch. A smile creeps across my face.

The kiss was better than I imagined. All these years, I've waited for Travis to kiss me. I've not let another man get close. I'm a twenty-four year old virgin. Stupid I know, but I've saved myself for him, for the only man I've ever wanted to touch me.

It seemed too easy to give it to someone else. I thought I'd meet someone who made me feel the way Travis does. But after working plenty of bars, I haven't met anyone I want to be intimate with.

Buzz Buzz

Travis's phone vibrates from the table where it's sitting.

A text from my brother lights up the screen.

You're keeping an eye on Kendra, right?

I want a full report.

I stare at the words, and my chest tightens. Travis has only been so attentive because Quentin asked him to be.

My stupid girlish fantasy got away from me. Thinking he's sitting at the bar watching me because he's attracted to me, but he's only watching me because my brother asked him to keep an eye on me.

He hit that guy not to stand up for me, but because Quentin wants a full report and he'll need to tell him what he did to protect his little sister.

And here I am throwing myself at him, practically begging him to kiss me.

Embarrassment prickles my skin. I've been so stupid.

I'm a silly girl who doesn't know a damn thing about men. I'm not going to stick around to embarrass myself anymore.

Grabbing my purse from the locker, I head upstairs to my room.

5

TRAVIS

The black waitress uniform hugs Kendra's luscious hips. The curve of her ass is a mouthwatering sight. I take another sip of my coffee, but it doesn't quench my thirst.

It's been over twelve hours since I kissed Kendra's pouty lips. But the taste of her lingers, filling up my senses. The imprint of her lips on mine, the memory of her teeth tugging my lower lip sends heat skittering over my body and blood thundering in my ears.

I thought I could resist Kendra. I thought this thing between us was stoppable. But now that I've had a taste, I realize how naïve I've been.

The pull I have towards her is overwhelming. It's bigger than her or me or her brother. I want to feel those lips on mine again, and to hell with the consequences.

I've been sitting here watching her work for the last two hours with my laptop open in front of me. I'm supposed to be doing inventory, but there's no way in hell I can keep my eyes off this woman.

I'm mesmerized by her, by the way she moves with the tray in the air, making her hips sway, the smile that lights up her face when she speaks to customers, that damn strand of bright pink hair that falls over her eyes and that she keeps tucking behind her ear.

I want to take that hair, wrap it in my fist, tilt her neck back, and kiss the hell out of her.

When I came back to the office last night, Kendra was gone. I don't know what I would have done if she'd still been there. Claimed her in the office, probably.

There was something between us last night, something real. But today, Kendra's barely said hello. She's avoiding me.

Does she regret kissing me last night? Does she regret kissing an old man? There's only one way to find out.

The last of the lunch customers leave, and Kendra clears their table and resets it for dinner.

There're a few hours before Kendra's needed for

the night shift, and as she goes out to get her purse, I corner her in the hallway.

"Kendra."

She spins around and takes a small step back when she sees me, her hands going up as if pushing me away even as her eyes widen and her lips part.

My eyes dart to her plump lips, and my mind goes blank. All I can think about is kissing those peachy perfect creations.

"Did you want to see me?"

Her voice pulls me out of my fantasy, and I remember why we're here. "Get your coat."

Her eyes narrow, and she tilts her head. "Why?"

She doesn't trust me, or maybe she doesn't trust herself around me. The thought has my cock twitching.

"I'm taking you for a ride."

Her eyes go wide, and an adorable pink blush creeps up her neck. I chuckle, realizing what I just said.

"On my bike."

She turns away, embarrassed, and I love that her thoughts went to a dirty place.

"I haven't had lunch," she mumbles.

I know she hasn't, because I've been watching her all morning. While pretending to work, I've been following her every move. I can't help myself; I'm obsessed with this angel with the pink halo.

"I've packed a picnic." I hold up the bag of food I had Maggie prepare for me.

"Oh." Her mouth forms a perfect, dick-sized O, and I have to keep moving or she's going to notice the wood in my pants.

"Come on. I know a good spot."

She pulls her eyebrows together like she's going to protest, but I don't give her a chance. I grab her coat from the lockers and snatch the purse from her hands.

"Hey!"

She follows me down the corridor and out to the bright sunshine of the courtyard. It's a beautiful, crisp spring afternoon, the perfect day for a ride.

"Are you always this bossy?" she asks when she catches up to me.

We reach my bike, and I stash the picnic in the saddle bags and help her shrug on her coat. "Only when there's something I want."

"Oh," she says again.

Pink creeps up her neck, and it's adorable how quickly I can make her blush. But she takes the helmet when I hand it to her.

Me and Quentin always had bikes growing up, and she's ridden with her brother before. But this is the first time I've felt Kendra on the back of my bike. Her thighs pressed against mine cause my nerves to go into overdrive.

She holds the side of the seat, and I pry them off and place them around my waist.

"Hold onto me. It's safer."

Which is bullshit, but if she's on my bike, her arms are around me.

We head onto the road, and it's pure bliss. The sun on my face, the bike humming beneath me, and Kendra on the back. Life doesn't get much better than this.

The road snakes uphill into the mountains. On one side, the cliff falls away to a canopy of trees and the commercial pine forest below. On the other side, it's a steep bank and wild forest.

After about twenty minutes, I take a dirt road that leads to one of my favorite walks on the mountain. Five minutes later, the dirt road doesn't end as much as peter out, the track giving way to undergrowth and scattered bush.

There's no one else here, and that's what I like about this spot. Most tourists go to the other side of the mountain where the town of Hope is. It's close to the lake and the ski fields and numerous hiking trails.

On the Wild side, we've got the sawmill and the

forestry that feeds it, and beyond that pure wilderness.

The path isn't sign posted, and you won't find it on a tourist map. It's an old tracker path that only the locals know about.

Kendra slides off the bike and tugs the helmet off her head. She tosses her hair and runs her hands through it, letting the gold and pink locks fall back into place.

I must be staring, because she takes a strand of the pink and twists it in her fingers, making a face. "Pink seemed like a good idea in Kentucky."

"I like it."

I take the strand out of her fingers and tuck it behind her ear, loving the way she looks up at me all wide-eyed.

"Come on. The path's this way."

We set off through the undergrowth, and I pick up the faint track. As we walk, I probe Kendra about the last few years. I'm curious as to what she's been doing all this time and why she stayed away. As far as I know, Quentin's only seen her a handful of times when he visited her in whatever small town she was currently living in. I worried about her as much as he did.

"What were you doing in Kentucky?"

"Waitressing, mostly."

When I last saw Kendra, she had big dreams. She was going to go to college. She was going to study literature.

"What happened to college?"

"Life happened." She shrugs, and my heart breaks for her. For the innocent girl who's been through such pain.

We walk in silence for a while, listening to the noises of the forest. When Kendra speaks, she's so quiet I can barely hear her.

"After the accident, I couldn't focus. I didn't want to be away at college. It seemed so stupid, studying classic literature. What was the point? And all the stupid sororities and the drinking. I did one semester and gave up. I just didn't want to be there."

I can understand that. It was the same for me after the first tour in Iraq. When I came back and went into a bar and there were plenty of guys my age, young men getting wasted on tequila shots. It seemed so frivolous.

"You ever thought of going back to college?"

I want that for her. I want her to have her best life, not one that she fell into because of grief.

"Maybe, but not to study literature."

"You don't enjoy reading anymore?"

Kendra always had her head buried in a book.

Romance mostly, judging from the bare-chested men on the covers.

She laughs. "Are you kidding? Reading has been what's gotten me through the last few years. But I want to do something more meaningful than write romance."

"What do you want to do?"

"I'd like to study psychology, be a therapist. Help people in some way."

She says it shyly, like it's the first time she's expressed her wishes out loud. I take her hand, and she glances at me but doesn't pull away.

"You'd make a great therapist. You should do it."

She bites her lower lip and smiles. "Maybe I will."

The conversation moves to other things.

Kendra asks me all about the bar and the MC club. And it seems like no time has passed before we reach the clearing.

There's a break in the canopy where sunlight filters in, and I spread the picnic blanket on the forest floor under the warm rays. Kendra plops down next to me, her short skirt riding up her thighs.

I grab the food and hand her a sandwich.

"You like chicken sandwiches?"

She takes it and we talk as we eat, the conversation flowing easily.

Maggie packed a large piece of apple pie and we share it, taking turns at scooping it up with a bamboo fork.

When we're done eating, Kendra lays back on the blanket and exhales deeply.

"I can see why you come here. It's peaceful."

Her hair fans out over the picnic blanket, and her eyes close.

I prop myself up on one elbow, drinking in the sight of her. For a long time, neither of us speaks. We listen to the bird sounds, and I watch her breathing.

One of her eyes peeps open and then narrows when she sees me watching her. "You don't have to take Quentin's instructions quite so literally."

I frown at her, not sure what she's talking about. "What do you mean?"

She props herself up on her elbows and looks at me.

"I know he told you to watch over me while he's away. And that's why you're in the bar when I'm working and why you've taken me out today."

Her words cut me. She thinks I'm only here because Quentin asked me to keep an eye on her.

"And I'm sorry I threw myself at you last night. It was silly. I was caught up in the moment…"

She trails off and looks down, a telltale blush

creeping up her neck. She brings her arm up to smooth her hair, and I catch it in mid-air.

"Quentin's got nothing to do with it," I growl. "I brought you here because I want to spend time with you. And I kissed you last night because I've been wanting to kiss you for the last six years."

"Oh." Her mouth pops open. "So this has got nothing to do with my brother?"

At her mention of Quentin, I sit up and run my hand through my hair.

"No. The only worry about your brother is what he'd think if he knew how much I want to kiss his little sister."

She sits up, breathing hard, and crawls over to me. "Do you want to kiss me?"

From my position above her, I can see right down her T-shirt. Her chest heaves up and down as she breathes. My gaze darts to her plump lips, begging to be kissed.

"Yes." My voice sounds husky with desire. "I'd very much like to kiss you."

I grab her by the shoulders and press my mouth to hers. She moans as our lips collide.

She tastes like apple pie and cinnamon. Her body presses towards mine, and then I'm pushing her gently back onto the blanket.

She falls back and I pin her hand above her head, getting tangled in her hair.

"Kendra." I breathe her name into her neck, kissing her delicate skin, tasting her throat and neck and moving back to her waiting lips. "I've been wanting to do this for a very long time."

She moans as my hand slides over her tummy and up to her breasts, and I palm one as my finger flicks across her nipple.

"Travis…" Her voice comes out needy and small.

"What is it, angel?"

"Is this really happening? I've crushed on you since I was eighteen."

I smile at her confession, glad I'm not the only one who imagined this moment.

"Oh, it's happening, angel."

My lips find hers, and there's a new hunger to our kiss. Kendra's body writhes under me, and my hard-on bumps against her softness.

I've tasted her lips. Now I want to taste her most intimate places. My hand slides up her skirt, and she gasps as I reach her panties. My fingertips trail over the damp fabric.

"You're wet for me, angel."

She bites her bottom lip. "You have no idea."

My fingers pull aside her panties, and I brush against her sensitive folds.

The little gasps and moans that come out of her mouth make me wild with desire. But I'll take my time with her. I've waited so long for a taste of Kendra. Now I shuffle down on the blanket until my lips find the soft skin of her inner thigh.

"What are you doing?" Her head lifts off the blanket to look at me anxiously.

I give her a wicked smile. "I think you know exactly what I'm doing."

She bites her lower lip and gives me a cute look halfway between embarrassment and desire.

"Lie down," I tell her. "I'm going to take care of you."

"You're so bossy," she says. But she lies back on the blanket.

I slide her panties down her silky thighs and over her feet. Once I have them off, I bring them to my nose and inhale. The musky smell of her arousal makes my dick ache.

I stuff her panties in my pocket and dip my head between her thighs, throwing her skirt up to her waist. Kendra gasps as the cool air hits her pussy.

I sit back and look at her, my beautiful pink angel. Her hair is splayed out like a halo, and she's got a dreamy look in her eyes.

I put a hand on each thigh and push them apart.

She opens up for me, revealing her perfect pink cunt.

"God, you're beautiful."

My hand stays on her pussy as I lower my head, and my lips brush her sensitive spot.

She bucks at the contact.

"Travis… "

I love the way she says my name, all whiny with need.

"What is, angel?"

"It feels too good. It's too much."

"Do you want me to stop?" I let my hot breath run over her pussy, and she shudders.

"No."

I chuckle. "Good. I'm not gonna stop until you scream my name."

My lips kiss her tender folds, and with every kiss she bucks her hips. Her nerves are pulled so tight, it won't take long to give her a release. Juice flows out of her pussy, and I press my tongue against her to lick her up.

She moans my name, and her hands clasp the back of my head.

Her pussy grows wetter as I lick and suck, keeping it slow and gentle, not quite giving her what she wants.

"Travis..."

It comes out as a whiny little whisper that drives me wild. Her hips buck, and she pulls my head towards her.

"Travis," she whines again, "what if someone comes?"

I lift my head and look around at the forest around us, the birdsong and the wind rustling the trees. Kendra's eyes meet mine, and they're full of desire and also anxious.

"Then I'll have to shoot them."

She giggles. But I'm only half joking.

I brought Kendra here because no one else knows about this spot. But if anyone saw this beautiful sight that I'm seeing now, I would have to kill them. No one sees my woman apart from me.

"Relax," I command, and she lies back on the blanket.

My thumb strums her clit as I slide my index finger into her tight little cunt. The walls of her pussy clench my finger. And she's so tight it makes me wonder if she's done this before. But that's a question I'll ask another time.

The thought thrills me. I want to be her first, and I want to be her last. But right now, I just want to make my angel come.

I slide my finger slowly in and out, loving the way she writhes under me. My tongue licks her clit, and I stretch my hand out until my pinky grazes her other little hole.

"Travis." She sits up in surprise, but there's desire in her look.

"Relax," I tell her. "I'm taking care of you."

She lays back down, and I go back to her sweet pussy. My tongue licks her from hole to hole and she grabs my hair, mewling my name.

"Keep saying my name, angel. I want you to say my name as you come. I want you to scream it. Let the entire forest know who's taking care of you."

She's panting hard, and I know it won't take me long now. I've drawn this out as long as I can, and as much as I love being down here, I want to give my girl a release. My speed picks up, strumming, sucking, licking, and finger fucking.

Her hips are bucking, and her hands are tugging at my hair. She writhes her hips, grinding her pussy into my mouth, and I push her hard, giving her everything she needs, licking her up and devouring her pussy like a mad man.

She screams my name as her pussy clenches, tugging at my fingers as juice cascades over my tongue.

I keep my mouth pressed to her, and just as she starts to come down, I start back up.

It doesn't take much to make Kendra come again. A little pressure from my mouth, a little twirl of my finger, and she's coming all over my tongue, grabbing my head with legs stuck straight up in the air.

She screams my name, and a flock of birds fly up from the trees and scatter into the sky.

But I don't let her rest. When one orgasm finishes, I move my mouth and she whimpers against me. I keep going, giving her everything she needs and more. Letting Kendra know I can look after her. That what she needs is an older man who knows how to take care of his woman.

I lose count of the number of times she comes, but finally her body goes limp. She lies back on the picnic blanket panting, her face sweaty and red and content.

"Travis." Every new way she says my name is a revelation. I thought screaming it as she came was the best, but whispering it in wonder comes pretty damn close. "I had no idea I could feel that good."

"Have something to drink, angel." I press the bottle of water to her lips, and she takes a few sips before collapsing back onto the blanket.

I take the panties out of my pocket and use them to mop up the pussy juice on her thighs. Then I stash them back in my pocket. They're coming home with me.

I lay down next to my angel.

"Kendra…"

There are so many questions I want to ask her. Is she sticking around? Can she ever be mine? But there's no response. My angel has fallen asleep.

6

KENDRA

The last two days have been the happiest of my life.

I've spent the days working at the restaurant and any spare time hanging out with Travis.

I was worried that he would think I was childish, still the teenage girl he knew before. But we talk easily about everything and anything. You don't notice the ten years' difference between us. Or at least, I don't.

We sneak off so the other guys in the MC suspect nothing. If my brother found out, he'd flip, and Travis doesn't want anyone telling him before he gets back.

I'm sure once Quentin sees how happy we are he'll be cool with us being together.

But it's not my brother I'm thinking of when

Travis gets his wicked tongue on me. He does things with his mouth and hands that make me lose control in the best way. And I've learned to work his cock with my hands the way he likes. But we haven't gone all the way.

There's a niggling question in the back of my mind. I'm not experienced with men. I kept my distance when I was on the road. I don't know if what we're doing is casual or not. It doesn't feel casual to me, but what would I know?

We're finishing the washing up after the dinner he made, spaghetti and meatballs with a delicious homemade sauce.

Every night, Travis drops me at home under darkness so nobody sees. He says he's not ready to tell people yet. We have to tell Quentin first about us.

With the dishes all done, it's late and almost time to go. Travis leans on the kitchen counter.

"I guess I better drop you at home."

I'm not ready to go home yet. I take a step toward him, and he puts his arms around me, pulling me in close.

"Can I stay?"

Travis groans. "I would love for you to stay. But there's a way to do this. I can't disrespect your brother. I need to speak to him first."

I know it makes sense, but try telling my heart that.

I wiggle my hips against his, making him groan. My pussy dampens at the guttural noise coming from his throat. I'm not ready to go home just yet, and feeling bold, I pull my top off. His gaze roams hungrily over my breasts.

I pull his top off too and walk my fingers slowly down the hard muscles of his chest. When I get down to his belt, I slowly undo the belt buckle.

Travis has been taking care of me with his mouth. I want to return the favor.

"What are you doing, angel?" He growls a warning as I sink to my knees, sliding his belt out of its grooves.

"Oh, I think you know what I'm doing."

My hand runs over the bulge in his jeans, and I apply some pressure. Travis groans as I undo the zipper.

"You don't have to do that, angel."

"I know. I want to do it."

I slide his jeans and boxers over his hips and his cock pops out, hard and ready. I lick my lips at the glorious sight and push him back against the kitchen counter. My hands grip the base of his shaft and I hesitate, not sure what to do.

"I've never done this before."

His gaze meets mine, his eyes hooded with desire. "Have you done any of this before, Kendra?"

He means sex. Not that we've had penetration, but we've done a hell of a lot in the last few days. I shake my head.

"I was waiting for you, Travis." He groans, a tortured look on his face that makes me feel powerful, knowing I can bring a strong man to his knees. "I'm a virgin. I want you to be my first."

"Angel…"

It comes out as a low, tortured moan. A drop of precum shoots out the end of his dick, and I duck my head and lick the pearly bead up with my tongue. His cock jerks my hands.

I glance up at him, wondering if I'm doing something right. Travis is watching me, and he gives an encouraging nod.

"You look good on your knees, angel. Take care of your man."

His words give me power, and I press my tongue to the base of his shaft and lick slowly upwards. He tastes salty and manly, and one lick gets my juices flowing.

My mouth experiments, licking and kissing his shaft and sliding my tongue around his tip. I slide him into my mouth, and his dick bumps up against my teeth. He's so big I have to slacken my jaw and stretch my mouth open wide. Even then, my mouth only comes halfway down his shaft.

I love watching his dick glisten as I take him in and out of my mouth. I glance upwards and Travis is watching me, his eyes dark with desire.

"That's it, angel. Take my cock into your mouth."

I keep sucking, loving his commands.

I suck and lick and tug and kiss. My teeth scrape against his skin, and it's sloppy and slobbery, but by the way he's moaning, I must be doing something right.

Then he grabs the back of my head. "Open your throat, angel."

He's bossing me around, and I like it. He grabs the back of my hair and slides my head down his shaft. I feel like my eyes are going to bug out of my head and I gag, but then I do as he says. My throat opens, and his cock grazes my tonsils.

He's in so deep, and when he groans with plea-sure my pussy aches.

My jaw drops right open, and my lips rub up and down his shaft as he pulls my head up and down him. My fingers cup his balls and I slide one finger around to his back passage, playing with his puck-ered hole the way he does with mine.

"Fuck Kendra."

The surprise in his voice makes me wet and needy.

"That's it." His voice is strained and croaky. "Good girl, Kendra. Good girl."

I know I'm doing a sloppy job. It's my first time. But the way he's moaning makes me feel powerful.

His fist twists in my hair. Then he pulls my head down and suddenly he's got control. He's fucking my mouth, and it's so damn sexy.

I love that I'm pleasing him, even though it feels like my jaw is about to drop off. I keep going, sucking and licking and moving my head where he pulls me.

My tits are bouncing up and down, straining at my pink lacey bra. And he's watching them as he pulls himself into my mouth.

"You're so sexy, Kendra. So damn sexy. I'm gonna come all over your tits."

Oh god. It's so dirty that new heat floods my pussy, and I'm aching for some friction down there but I've got both hands on his cock.

I feel his cock thicken. Then he rips it out of my mouth and grabs the base of his cock. Hot liquid hits my tits and splashes onto my face as he sprays cum on my chest.

Cum trickles over my skin and I'm panting, hot and wet. He sees my need and drops to his haunches, pulling me onto the wooden floor with him.

"You need taking care of, angel."

I whimper as he throws up my skirt and tugs my wet panties off. With his other hand, he swirls his cum all over my chest.

"You're mine."

The words only make me more needy. I find his cock, and he's already hard again.

"Fuck me, Travis," I whimper.

For the last two days we've fooled around a lot, but we haven't been all the way. Now I'm crazy with desire and want his cock in me.

He growls. But he doesn't give me what I need.

His cock presses against my thigh, and it's so fucking close.

"No, angel. I won't claim you yet."

Disappointment courses through me, and I grab his cock and pull it towards me.

But his hand gets there first. He thrusts two fingers into my dripping pussy. I'm so needy that it only takes two pumps before I come on his palm.

The release is intense and I press myself to him, our bodies covered in each other's juices. He moves his fingers again and I tug his cock. Then he's coming with me, hot cum squirting onto my thigh.

I give a frustrated cry. I want him in me so bad.

"Not yet, Kendra." He kisses me gently. "I will claim you soon. I will take that sweet cherry of yours, but you have to be patient, angel. This has to be done right."

He's thinking of my brother again and what Quentin would do to him if he found out what Travis has been up to with his little sister. It makes sense to wait, but I don't see how coming on my tits is any less disrespectful than making love.

But I'm too tired to argue. Travis scoops me up and takes me to his bedroom. He washes me down with a warm flannel and climbs into bed next to me.

Every night, he's taken me back to the clubhouse on his bike. But tonight we sleep together, wrapped tight in each other's arms.

7

TRAVIS

*K*endra sleeps like she comes, all in. Her hair's spread over the pillows, her mouth hangs open emitting soft snores, her legs are tangled in the bed sheets, and she's taking up way more than half the bed.

A feeling of contentment spreads over me as I watch her. I could get used to this.

It's only been a few days that we've been together, but it's been a lifetime that I've wanted this woman.

She's frustrated because we haven't gone all the way, but we've got a lifetime together. Why rush? Besides, I need to speak to Quentin first, out of respect for my best friend and MC brother.

And there's something else I want to do. I want Kendra to know how serious I am. While she's working today, I'm taking a ride across the mountain to Hope. There's a boutique jewelry shop there, and I'm going to buy her a ring.

I don't want her running off again. I want her to be here, tied to me as my fiancé. Once I've got a ring on her finger, I'll tell her brother. Then I'll claim her. And I'll put a baby in her belly and keep her tied to me for good.

Kendra stirs and I hate to wake her, but I need to drop her back at the club while it's still early. I hate sneaking around like this, but it's only for one more day, and the last thing I want is the rumor mill starting before I've spoken to Quentin.

I slip out of bed and get the coffee going, then wake up my angel with a fresh brew.

"Morning, angel."

Kendra grunts and sits up in bed, reaching for the coffee with her eyes half closed. She's not a morning person.

Dawn's breaking over the crest of the mountain as we ride to the compound. As soon as she's got a ring on her finger, she'll be staying at my place permanently. But for now, I return her to the room above the bar.

Kendra heads upstairs, probably to go back to sleep, while I head to the office.

I spend the next few hours catching up on inventory, my mind wandering to Kendra and making it hard to focus. I wonder if I'll stop obsessing about her once we're engaged and I know she's mine.

The morning shift comes in, and I chat with Arlo. Maggie walks past, and I notice his eyes following her. She's proving indispensable in the kitchen, and I hope he doesn't do anything to make her want to leave. It's hard enough finding staff to stick around.

Kendra comes down to start her lunch shift. She's had a shower and her hair is tied back off her face, which is radiant. She smiles at me, and I resist the urge to kiss her.

Soon. Soon I'll let every motherfucker in this place know that she's mine. But not till I've told Quentin first.

I'm about to take my laptop out to the bar so I can keep an eye on Kendra when I hear the roar of bikes pulling into the compound. I head to the window as four Wild Riders pull into the courtyard. It's Quentin and Prez and the two other guys who went with them. I frown. They're not meant to be back for two more days.

Two more days that I had to convince Kendra to marry me and stay on the mountain.

The phone rings in the office, and I head back inside. It's a query about one of our orders, and I deal with it quickly. I'm about to hang up when Quentin appears in the door frame.

"Hey, brother."

He's staring at me, and I wonder if there's some way that he knows. Me and Kendra have been discreet, but maybe someone saw us. Then he slaps me on the back and grins.

"You're back early. What happened?"

Quentin fills me in on the meetings they had with new distributors and the ones that were cancelled because of flooding in the area. Entire roads were closed, and they cut their losses and came back. We'll have to arrange the meetings for another time.

With business talk out the way, Quentin pulls on his beard and looks at me intently. "How's Kendra? Anything I need to know?"

8

KENDRA

*M*y stomach twists at the sound of bikes roaring into the compound. Quentin's back. Travis will tell him about us, and we can stop sneaking around. Our relationship will be public, and I won't have to get up at some godawful time in the morning just so no one sees us.

"Could you grab me some more napkins?" Arlo asks.

He's been on every shift with me and Travis and must know there's something between us, but he keeps his expression neutral, and I hope he's discreet long enough for Travis to speak to Quentin first.

I check the station, and we're all out of napkins.

"I'll get some from out back." It's a quiet shift, and they won't miss me for a moment.

The supply closet is down the corridor next to

the office, and as I approach, I hear the low rumble of Quentin and Travis talking.

Butterflies beat in my chest. What if they're talking about me? I shake the thought out of my head. It's their conversation to have in private. Opening the door to the supply cupboard, I grab the napkins and shut it quietly.

I'm about to head back to the restaurant when I hear my name.

"How's Kendra?" asks Quentin.

I pause to listen. It's not eavesdropping if you're the topic of conversation, right?

"Anything I need to know about?"

I clutch my throat as the butterflies inside me beat against my chest. This is the moment that Travis tells my brother about us. That he tells him we're in love and we're going to be together. Then Quentin will slap him on the back and tell him he always wanted him to be part of the family. They'll have a beer together and Travis will kiss me in front of his club, claiming me as his old lady. And all my teenage fantasies will come true.

Except that's not what Travis says. "She's doing okay," he says.

My heart stops beating for a moment.

She's doing okay.

What the hell does that mean? I was doing more

than okay. When I had his cock in my mouth last night, he was singing my praises like I was a goddess.

"Nothing to report," says Travis.

"Thanks for keeping an eye on her," Quentin says. "I know it can't have been fun watching my kid sister."

Travis mumbles something that I can't make out. But I've heard enough.

Nothing to report.

He was supposed to tell Quentin about us. Tell him we love each other and want to be together. Unless that's not what he wants? He's never said those words. We've messed around, and he's told me I'm sexy and beautiful and made me come so many times I lost count. But he's never told me this is forever.

The reality comes crashing down on me. I've been so stupid. I'm his best friend's kid sister. My stupid teenage fantasies have run away with me again.

Of course Travis wouldn't be interested in a pink-haired girl who's barely out of her teens. He was tasked with babysitting me and thought he'd have some fun along the way. That's why he didn't want anyone to see us. That's why he didn't want to go all the way. Because this isn't some teenage romance. This is real life, and in real life, men suck.

I've been so stupid. I shouldn't have come back.

There's movement in the office, and I quickly dart out of the way.

I take the door at the end of the corridor that leads upstairs. Going quickly and quietly, I throw off my apron and chuck it over the end of the bed. My stuff doesn't take long to pack. Then I sling my duffel bag over my shoulder and take the fire escape that leads to the side of the courtyard. Nobody sees me as I drop to the ground.

I keep to the shadows until I'm past the compound. Then I walk quickly down the mountain road away from the restaurant, away from the Wild Riders MC, and away from Travis.

It's a few miles to Wild where I can get a bus to Hope and then a train to wherever the hell gets me out of here the quickest. Unless I get a ride first. Once I get around the corner, I stick out my thumb.

Life on the road is uncomplicated. There's only myself to look out for and no stupid heart to get in the way. It was a mistake to come here.

9

TRAVIS

*a*s Quentin talks to me about the meetings, my mind becomes more agitated. I don't enjoy lying to him about Kendra. The sooner I can get out of here and buy her the ring, the better. I'm about to make my excuses when Arlo comes in from the bar.

"You guys seen Kendra?"

At the sound of her name, my head jerks up. There's a tone to Arlo's voice that I don't like.

"She's in the restaurant, isn't she?"

Arlo shakes his head. "She went to get napkins twenty minutes ago, and I haven't seen her since."

I glance at Quentin, and he's scowling at Arlo.

"What do you mean you haven't seen her?"

"She didn't come back to finish her shift. It's not like her."

Kendra's only been working at the restaurant for a week, but she's reliable. I push my chair back and stand up, my heart hammering in my chest.

"She might be upstairs."

Quentin and I both bolt for the door, and I get there just ahead of him. I take the stairs two at a time and race to her room.

"Kendra." I bang on her door, and there's no answer. "Kendra!"

I push the door open and barge in. Her waitress apron lies on the bed, along with the branded t-shirt and black skirt that makes up her uniform.

"Shit."

I pull open the closet, and it's empty.

Quentin barges into the bathroom, but our search of the room reveals what my heart already knows. "She's gone."

I can't keep the despair out of my voice. I thought we had something real. I thought she felt the same about me as I do about her. I don't know why she would run.

Quentin tugs on his beard and turns his intense gaze on me.

"Why would she leave?"

I drag my gaze around the room, not wanting to meet his eye. I can't lie to him anymore.

"Travis…" His voice has a rough edge to it. "Why would Kendra leave?"

I meet his gaze, and his eyes are dark with suspicion. I suck in a deep breath and let it out slowly. I've got to tell him.

"Is there something I need to know, Travis?"

Quentin takes a step towards me. They don't call him Barrels for nothing. It's not only because he runs the brewery. The man's thick and stocky, built like a barrel.

I put my hand up in the air in a placating gesture.

"It's not what you think."

That's the wrong thing to say. Because Quentin's expression goes from suspicion to fury in two seconds flat.

"What the fuck, man? Have you been fucking my sister?"

I wince at the harsh words. "It's not like that."

"So something is going on between you?"

He tugs at the side of his mouth and jostles his feet. I know what's coming before he swings the punch. I dodge his fists, and he comes at me again.

"Fuck you, man. She's my sister."

He lunges at me and we go barreling into the dresser, bringing the mirror crashing to the ground.

"It's not like that."

We tumble to the floor, and I roll away out of his grasp.

Quentin is a big guy, and I'm faster than him so I can dodge his fists, but I won't fight back. If he hits me, then I fucking deserve it. This is a shitty thing to do to your best friend.

I scramble to my feet and Quentin faces me, breathing hard.

"I love her, man."

His eyes narrow.

"I don't give a shit. You don't touch my sister." He comes at me again and I dodge out the way, but he clips my shoulder. A flash of pain shoots down my arm, and I stagger backwards.

"I love her." I say it louder. And it feels damn good to say it.

Quentin swivels around and swings at me again, and I dive under his arm and skip backwards across the room.

"Listen to me, Quentin. I love Kendra. I'm going to marry her. I was waiting for you to get back to tell you."

"You want to marry Kendra?"

The talk of marriage stops him. He's breathing hard, bent over with his hands on his knees, and we stare at each other across the room.

He's like a raging bull, and I don't know if he's going to charge. I don't give him a chance.

"I tried to deny my feelings, man. But I love her. She's the most amazing, smart, funny, kind, caring woman I've ever met. I want to make her my wife. I want to do right by her."

He's breathing heavily as he stares at me, the words sinking in.

We've been through a lot of together, me and Quentin. We fought alongside each other; we've seen shit a man shouldn't see. We've been through hell and back, and we've ridden together to chase the demons out of our lives.

It's only because he knows me so well that I'm still standing right now.

"She feel the same way about you?"

My shoulders sag with relief that he's coming around to the idea.

"I don't know," I say honestly. "I hope so. I was going to buy her a ring today and find out. I'm not messing around with her, Quentin. This is for keeps."

"This is a lot take in." He lets out a big sigh and runs his hands through his hair.

"But if she loves you, why the fuck has she gone?"

His words have me racing for the door. "I don't know. But I'm gonna find her and find out."

We've wasted time fighting and Kendra could be miles away, picked up in some stranger's car. The thought has me bolting down the stairs.

I hear Quentin running behind me as I sprint to my bike.

"I'm coming too. I don't know what the fuck has gone on between you two, but if she's running away from you, it can't be fucking good."

His words have a grim warning to them. I wanted to get his blessing, but we're a long way from that.

I push the thought out of my head as I gun the engine. I can't let Kendra leave the mountain. I have to find her.

10
KENDRA

There's a blister forming on my left heel. I should put my sneakers on, but in my haste to get the hell away from the Wild Riders clubhouse, I pulled on my knee-high boots. The heel on them means they're not made for walking long distances, but in the half hour I've been on the road, I've seen only two cars.

These remote mountain roads aren't good for hitchhikers.

The goddamn birds are singing too loud and the sun blasts my face, making me squint. But I can't waste time stopping to get my sunglasses out of my bag. I want to put as much distance between me and Travis as possible.

How could I be so stupid as to think there was anything real between us? It's my stupid teenage fantasies where we get together and live happily ever after messing with my head. I thought I was playing them out, but he was just playing with me.

I don't think Travis meant to play me. He's an older man and probably has affairs with women all the time. I'm just too inexperienced with men to realize that's all it was.

Travis never promised me anything. It was all me that put that on us, wanting to believe in my teenage fantasy.

But that just makes it harder. If Travis was an asshole, at least I could feel angry. But all I feel is a deep sadness, a heaviness in my chest. It's a heaviness that makes it hard to put one blistered foot in front of the other. It'll take me another hour to get to town. And then I'm changing shoes, getting on the bus, and never coming back.

An engine roars somewhere behind me, and I step to the side of the road and stick my thumb out, waiting for the car to come around the corner.

But it's not a car. It's a motorbike, and it screeches to a halt beside me, kicking up gravel and dust into my eyes.

"I thought I told you not to hitchhike."

Travis slides off his bike and saunters toward me like a protective big brother. Still watching out for me like Quentin asked him to.

I drop my bag in the dirt and put my hands on my hips. Now I'm glad I'm wearing my knee high boots because they make me look like a tough bitch, even though inside I feel like a silly schoolgirl in love.

If he's come to lecture me, I won't show him any vulnerability.

But as he strides over to me, the concern in his eyes almost makes me crumble. Almost. I remember the words that he said to Quentin.

Nothing to report.

I'll give him nothing to report. He'll know nothing of my feelings. I stick my chin out, ready to go into battle, but instead he cups it in his hand and pulls my face toward his. I'm speechless as his thumb strokes my cheek. "Don't leave, Kendra."

His eyes search mine, and my resolve crumbles. The tears I've been fighting back bubble to the surface and I squeeze my eyes shut, not wanting him to see how much I'm hurting.

"Don't go, Kendra," he says. "I want you to stay."

With my eyes squeezed shut, I can't see his face. I think about everything that's gone on between us. His reluctance to go all the way, the sneaking around so no one sees, and then not telling my brother when he had the chance. Anger bubbles to the surface, and I pull away and out of his grasp.

"So you can keep sneaking around with me as your fuck buddy?"

He stumbles backwards as if I've slapped him.

"No, it's not like that."

"Isn't it? Because it feels like you're embarrassed to be with me."

He's got a horrified expression on his face, and he's shaking his head.

"No. Kendra, you can't think that."

Another bike rolls around the corner, and Quentin comes into view. He slams on the brakes and pulls up behind us. He's off the bike and striding over, not bothering to take his helmet off.

"Are you fucking hitchhiking?"

I roll my eyes at my over-protective big brother. "It's the quickest way to get off this damn mountain."

Travis flinches at the words and looks wounded.

"Is it because of this asshole?" Quentin stands between us and jerks his thumb at Travis. I've never seen him angry at his best friend before. "He tells me he loves you, but there's got to be a reason you're leaving. If he's done anything to hurt you, I swear to God I will ruin that pretty face of his."

Quentin paces in anger, and as he talks he points an angry finger at Travis. But my brain got stuck when he used the "L" word.

My gaze darts to Travis and he's staring at me, his expression hurt and anxious.

"It's true. Angel, I love you. I'm not sneaking around because I'm embarrassed. It's because I respect your brother, and I wanted his blessing. But I see now that was a mistake. I love you, Kendra. I always have."

He takes my hand, and my resolve melts away. Our eyes lock and I search his, looking for the truth.

Quentin growls.

"Is this what you want, Kendra? Is this really what you want? If he's forced himself on you, if he's hurt you in any way... I don't care if he's my best friend. He'll be off this mountain and out of your life with a broken face."

I look between both men. Both of them showing their love for me in different ways. My heart fills with joy at how lucky I am. To have these two men looking out for me, my overprotective brother and the man I love, with a code of honor that I don't understand.

"Yes. That's what I want."

Travis reaches behind me and snaps a pine needle from a tree.

"This isn't how I was planning it, but I want you both to know how serious I am."

He drops to his knees in the gravel as he twists

the pine needle into a circle. I gasp as I realize what he's about to do.

Travis glances at Quentin who's as wide-eyed as I am.

"Could you give us a moment here, man?"

Quentin steps back, and Travis turns back to me.

"Kendra, I've loved you since the day I turned up for Thanksgiving at your house. I've carried your photo in my wallet for the last six years. It's your face I turned to during the dark times. When I was in Iraq and it felt like hell, I would pull out that photo and think of you. Sorry if my stupid honor kept me from doing this sooner. I was gonna buy a ring today, but if this is what I have to do to get you to stay on the mountain, then this will have to do. Will you make me the most fulfilled man alive and marry me?"

The butterflies explode out of my chest and come rushing out in a joyful, "Yes!"

I throw my arms around Travis, and he spins me around and around until I'm dizzy. He sets me down on the ground, and there's a broad grin on his face.

We're both laughing, and I glimpse Quentin watching us with a frown.

"Do I have your blessing?" Travis asks.

Quentin runs his hand through his hair. "It's a lot

to get used to. I need some time. But if my sister has to marry someone, I guess I'm glad it's you."

Knowing my brother, that's about the biggest blessing we're ever going to get.

Travis slaps him on the back. "Thanks, man."

Suddenly, my feet lift off the ground as Travis scoops me into the air. I throw my arms around his neck as he kisses me hard.

Quentin scowls. "You're not married yet."

I throw him a look. "Can you take my bag? There's no room on the bike for it."

Quentin shakes his head and mumbles curses. But he picks up the bag and straps it to the back of his bike as I take my place behind Travis.

"Are we going back to work?"

"No." He shakes his head. "We're going to my cabin. You've been driving me crazy all week, Kendra. It's time to claim what's mine.

A shiver of anticipation goes through my body. The vibration of the bike rumbles under me, and heat gushes between my legs as we race back up the mountain. I am ready to be claimed.

11
TRAVIS

*D*ust from the road kicks up behind us as we speed up the mountain. I'm breaking every speed limit in the county, but I've got my girl, no, my fiancé behind me, and I'm not slowing down for anyone.

Kendra's arms are tight around me, and she rests her head on my back. Her body's pressed against mine, warming me up and filling me with anticipation of what's to come.

As soon as we pull up in front of my cabin, I cut the engine. She slides off the bike, and I lift her into my arms.

Kendra squeals, and her arms go around my neck. Her girlish giggle makes me feel like a young man again, energized and full of hope instead of hardened by war. I love that she makes me feel like that.

I unlock the cabin with one hand and carry her inside, kicking the door shut behind us.

"Hey, I've got a shift to finish." She wiggles in my arms.

"Nope. Not today."

The restaurant will have to cope without us for a few hours, because I've got plans for Kendra. I carry her into the bedroom and sit her down on the edge of the bed.

"I don't want people to think I'm getting special treatment because I'm sleeping with the boss."

She's teasing me, giving me some sass, and I love it. But before she can say anything else I press my mouth to hers, quieting that sassy mouth for a while.

I put my hands on her thighs and sit back, crouching on the floor before her.

"That sassy mouth is going to get you in trouble one day."

She gives me a cheeky smile. "I hope so."

The look she's giving me makes all the blood rush to my dick. I've had a permanent hard-on ever since she walked into my bar, and now it's time to do something about it.

Kendra's wearing sexy knee-high boots, and as I crouch between her thighs, the leather scrapes my skin, sending heat coursing through my body, and dirty ideas spring into my mind.

She leans forward to unzip her boot, and I stop her hand.

"These are staying on."

Her mouth pops open, and I chuckle as her surprised look turns to curiosity. I slide a hand up her skirt and caress the gusset of her panties. They're dripping wet, and the moan that escapes her lips lets me know how ready she is for this.

"You're wet for me. Good girl."

"I've been wet for you ever since I was eighteen." She leans back on the bed, propped up by her elbows. "All I ever wanted was for you to take my cherry."

She bites her bottom lip and gives me an innocent look like she's that eighteen year old girl again.

"Keep talking, angel. Tell me about that teenage fantasy of yours."

She bows her head and peeps out at me from lowered lashes.

"You might think I'm silly."

"I doubt that, angel. You're sexy as hell." My fingers brush her panties, and she gasps. "Now tell me the fantasy."

She smiles. "You're as bossy in my fantasies as you are in real life."

"Oh yeah? What do I tell you to do?"

She bites her lower lip, and she takes a while to get the words out. It's not until I press my thumb against her panties and rub her clit that she opens her mouth.

"First, you tell me to take my panties off." Her voice comes out breathless, and the more she talks the harder I get.

I hook my thumbs under the top of her panties, and she lifts her hips so I can slide them off. She sticks her legs out, and I take them right over the top of those sexy leather boots and drop them on the floor.

"Then what?" My voice comes out raspy. But I'm so turned on by her teenage fantasy, to know this is what she wanted and now I can give it to her.

"Then you would tell me to undress."

I tug at her skirt until it's on the floor. Then I pull her t-shirt over her head. Her perfect breasts are bursting out of a pink lacy bra. She's a vision, leaning back on the bed with nothing but her bra and boots on. But I want to see more. I want to see all of her.

"Take your bra off, angel."

I set an edge to my voice to make it commanding, and a shiver goes through her. I sit back on my haunches to watch her undress herself.

Her hands slip around and unhook the bra and she crosses her arms and eases the straps off her shoulders, pulling the bra slowly off until her beautiful round globes are free.

Just the sight of those pink nipples standing on end has me hard as a rock. I want to plunge myself between those breasts. I want to run my dick over every part of this woman. But I'm a patient man, and I'm enjoying this exquisite torture.

"What happens next in your fantasy, angel?"

She gives me a shy smile. "Then I touch myself."

Her hand slides over her body and snakes up to her breasts. She cups a tit in one hand, and her thumb brushes over the nipple. She's biting her bottom lip, and as she works her nipple, her look turns from uncertainty to pure desire.

This may be a teenage girl's fantasy, but Kendra's all woman now.

"Now what?" I'm breathing hard, and I've never been so turned on.

"Then you touch me."

I bring my hand back to her pussy, and my fingers graze her sticky folds. But she shakes her head. The embarrassed girl is gone, and in front of me is a confident woman who knows what she wants.

"With your mouth."

I don't have to be told twice. I duck between her legs and hoist one thigh over my shoulder. The leather boot brushes against my skin, sending shivers all through me. My mouth presses to the soft skin of her leg just above the boot.

She gives a little whimper, and I look up.

"Keep playing with those gorgeous tits, angel. And don't stop until you're screaming my name."

She gasps at my command, but the good girl does as she's told.

I kiss her inner thigh, taking my time and enjoying the taste of her.

The closer I get to her musky core, the harder my heart pounds. With one hand I unzip my cock, needing to let the beast out.

"This is all for you, angel. You're gonna ride my cock in a minute. But first, I'm gonna get you warmed up."

My mouth goes back to the top of her thigh, inching towards her sticky core. She pushes her hips forward, trying to hurry me along. But I'm enjoying taking my time and making her squirm.

Finally, my lips brush her pussy opening and she whimpers. She's glistening wet, and I lick up all her juices as she quivers against me.

I glance up, and she's looking down at me as her hands tweak her nipples. I take my hand off my cock

SADIE KING

and I slide it between her folds, getting my finger nice and coated in pussy juice. Then I slide it into her.

She cries out and bucks her hips forward, taking every part of my finger. Her tight little pussy opens for me. In a moment, I'll have my cock in there. The thought drives me wild, and I plunge my fingers into her as I lick and suck. She throws her other leg over my shoulder, and leather rubs against the skin of my neck.

She shuffles her hips down the bed so that her legs wrap around me and the heels of her boots dig into my shoulders. I gasp as pricks of pain shoot through my body and straight to my dick. Precum spurts out of me, and I'm about to lose it without even getting inside her.

I roll my tongue over her clit, licking and sucking. She's panting hard, and then she's screaming my name as her pussy convulses.

I don't give her a chance to come down. I need to be inside Kendra, and I need it now.

I stand up and pull my jeans and boxers down in one movement.

Then I'm standing above her with my dick pointing straight at her tight little cunt. It's dripping and it's throbbing, and she licks her lips and edges forward, but I push her back.

"I'm getting inside that tight little pussy, angel, and I'm making you mine. I'm clean, and I'm not using a condom."

She nods. "Okay."

"Good. Because I'm gonna put my baby in your belly and tie you to me forever."

I climb between her thighs, and she scrambles back on the bed. I push her backwards and she bounces with the force of it, making her tits bump together. I lie on top of her, forcing her thighs apart with my legs. I'm being rough, but I can't stop.

My cock is taking over. I've seen her tight little cunt, that pink hole looking so inviting, and there's nothing I can do now to stop it.

"This might hurt for a minute, angel."

My gaze meets hers. It's taking all my restraint to hold back, but I need to let her know how I feel before I totally destroy her.

"I love you, Kendra." Emotion wells up inside me as I say it. She opens her mouth to speak, but I don't give her a chance. I thrust hard into that tiny little hole.

She screams and her thighs clutch me, the leather brushing my skin and driving me wild. I stay still inside her as her pussy clenches around me, and she's so tight it feels like she might squeeze my cock right off. Her eyes are shut tight, and I can't have that.

"Look at me, Kendra."

Her eyes open, and she holds my gaze as I slowly inch out of her. My cock's covered in her virgin blood and glistening juices.

"I love you. But I'm going to destroy you."

I pull my hips back and I thrust again, needing to pound this pussy. Needing to take out all my years of frustration, all the waiting, all the longing.

She had her youthful fantasies, but I had mine, and now I'm living them out as I pound into Kendra, her body bouncing like a rag doll with every thrust.

"I've imagined this for so long, angel."

Fucking my palm, thinking about her pussy, and now that I'm in her I'm like a man possessed.

But I want to go deeper.

I pull out, and she whimpers.

"Get on your knees."

She does as she's told like a good girl, and I kneel behind her and grab her hips.

My cock runs over her puckered back hole. One day soon I'll claim that too, but not today. Today I need the pussy I've been dreaming about for all these years.

I grab her ass and tilt her hips upwards, and there it is. Her pink pussy. So fucking gorgeous.

My cock twitches at the sight of her glistening hole, and I'm about to thrust into her when she surprises me by moving her hips back, sinking herself down my shaft.

A groan escapes me, and she moans at the same time.

"Fuck, Kendra."

I'm lost for words. I can't speak. The sensation is too great. I pull her back and forth down my cock, my thrusts getting harder and faster. She's bouncing up and down and the bed is jumping about and the springs can't last, but I can't be gentle. I can't slow this down; my need is too great.

My dick plunges in and out of her as my thumb brushes against her puckered asshole.

"Touch yourself."

I love commanding her, and like a good girl, she obeys.

Her hand reaches between her legs and she rubs her clit, her fingernails brushing against my balls. "Good girl, Kendra."

She glances over her shoulder, and her gaze meets mine.

My God, this woman means so much to me. In that look, I see love. I see my future. I see everything that's good in this world.

"Come for me, angel."

SADIE KING

Her eyes go wide, and her pussy clenches around me as she screams my name. My cock thickens and the animal inside me takes over and I'm fucking her so hard that her head's hitting the headboard. "Fuck, fuck, FUCK Kendra!"

Cum erupts out of me, and my entire body seems to explode. Thick ropes of seed slam into her pussy and I thrust, and I thrust, and I thrust until I'm spent. Everything I've saved up for her for the last six years, I let her have it.

When I pull my cock out of her, it's coated in her virgin blood and my sticky cum.

She flops down on the bed, and I collapse next to her. Only now does she slip off those goddamn sexy leather boots.

"My God, Travis." She's breathless. "That was unreal. Is it always like that?"

I pull her close to me and plant little kisses on her head.

"It's however we want to make it, angel. I had six years of cum, six years of waiting built up inside me that I had to give you. You'll hurt tomorrow, but next time I'll be gentler. I promise."

She gives me that shy smile. "What if I don't want it gentle?"

My cock hardens at her words.

"Angel, you can have it any way you want. We've got an entire lifetime to figure it out."

She nestles against me, content and happy, and her breathing soon becomes regular as she falls into sleep.

I pull the blanket over the both of us and hold her close. I got everything I ever wanted, and it's so much more than I ever expected.

EPILOGUE

KENDRA

One year later…

The scowl on Travis's face lets me know I'm in trouble even before he opens his mouth.

"I told you not to work today, angel."

I sling the apron over my head defiantly. The tie at the back almost doesn't come together over my round belly, but I manage to secure it.

"Jeez, Travis. It's only pregnancy. I can still work."

He rubs my belly. "I'd prefer it if you didn't."

"You're short on staff. It's a quiet lunch shift. I'm just going to wait a few tables for a couple of hours. There's nothing to worry about."

He looks uncertain. But then Maggie calls out a

food order, and I give him a kiss on the cheek and waddle off before he can tell me off again.

It's sweet how protective Travis has been since I got pregnant. But I wouldn't do anything to endanger the baby. I've cut my shifts back, not because of the pregnancy but because of my studies. I'm taking an online psychology course. It will be a few years of study doing it part time, but when I'm done, I'll be a qualified therapist.

With the scowl still on his face, Travis takes a seat at the bar. That's where he always works when I'm on shift. He says he thinks better there, but I know it's because he can keep an eye on me. My overprotective man. It makes me feel safe and cared for.

I'm taking a tray of drinks to a table when Quentin strides into the bar. He frowns at my stomach and takes the tray off me.

I give a long sigh.

"Jeez. Between the two of you, a girl can't do anything anymore."

He turns his frown on Travis. "What are you doing letting her work?"

Travis shrugs. "You ever try to stop your sister from doing something she really wants to do?"

Quentin still hasn't gotten used to the idea of us being together, even though we're married now.

We had a quiet ceremony in the Wild Chapel

officiated by the Prez. With so many of his MC getting married, he got himself ordained.

It was our MC family and some of our friends from the other side of the mountain. I've gotten to know the people on Wild Heart Mountain and the small but tight community who lives here.

I just wish that Quentin would accept me and Travis. He gave me away at the wedding, but he's still coming around to the idea.

With both of them scowling at me, I know when I'm beaten.

"Fine," I say. "One of you wait the tables. I'm going to fold napkins."

I undo the apron and hold it out to my two protectors. Travis and Quentin look at each other.

Travis takes the apron and throws it on the bar. "I'll cover the shift, but I'm not wearing an apron."

The phone behind the bar rings, and I'm closest so I grab it.

"Wild Taste Bar and Restaurant, Kendra speaking."

It's Joseph on the other end. He's known as Lone Star to the MC club because of his hermit nature. Of all the guys at the MC, he's the one I know the least. He only comes in for the weekly meetings and prefers his own company up in the woods.

"Are Kobe and Hailey up there?" he asks.

I've gotten to know the loved up couple from the other side of the mountain. They stop by often, although not as much since they had the baby.

"I haven't seen them. Hang on and I'll double check."

I glance around the restaurant, peering into the corners and the eating area across the road. Travis gives me a questioningly look.

"Have Hailey and Kobe been in today?"

He shakes his head. "Who wants to know?"

"Lone Star."

He takes the phone off me and holds it so we can both hear.

"They're away for the weekend. Went to the coast."

I share a look with Travis. It's unusual for Lone Star to call.

"I went up there to give Kobe some deer meat and found a girl on their doorstep. Says she's Hailey's sister."

I've heard Hailey talk about her older sister and how much she misses her.

"Is she okay?" I ask.

There's silence from Lone Star. Then I hear a baby crying.

"Is that a baby?" asks Travis.

"Yup. She's got a baby with her."

Me and Travis share a look, and I know without asking to offer to help.

"Are they okay? Does she need somewhere to stay?"

"She's fine," he says. "I'll take care of it."

He hangs up the phone, and Travis and I shrug at each other.

"I guess she'll get back in her car and head home."

"I hope he's not offering his place."

Travis says it as a joke, and we both laugh at the thought of the reclusive, monosyllabic Lone Star who likes peace and quiet with a baby in his house.

We're distracted by my own baby moving in my belly. A smile lights up my face, and I take Travis's hand and place it over my belly. A moment later he feels the kick, and a broad grin spreads across his face.

"I can't wait to meet this little guy."

"Me too."

He leans forward and kisses my lips, and a warm feeling encases my heart. I've got my man and a baby on the way. It's everything my teenage self ever wanted.

* * *

WHAT TO READ NEXT

A single mom in danger and the ex-military biker who becomes her protector...

I found her on the doorstep with a baby in her arms.

A woman on the run, as damaged as I am.

We each have our demons from the past. Mine are internal and harder to fight, remnants from my days in the military. But I can take on Trish's demons.

When her ex comes to claim her, he doesn't expect to find an entire MC club of hardened ex-military mountain men fighting her corner.

Because I'll do anything to protect my wild runaway.

Wild Runaway is a single-mom in danger, MC-lite steamy romance featuring an ex-military protector hero and the curvy woman who runs away with his heart.

WILD RUNAWAY

Josepth

The half a deer carcass in the back of the pickup bumps up and down as I drive over the uneven surface of the mountain road. I watch it in the rearview mirror, wondering if I should have strapped it down better or if it'll jump right out of the crate.

It's a fresh kill from today, and I'm making good on my promise to give a shank to Kobe. He's got a baby on the way, and I don't mind sharing my meat with others on the mountain who need it.

The private gravel road that leads to Kobe and Hailey's cabin is lined with tall pine trees and scraggly bushes that scrape against the pickup as I turn in.

The driveway opens up to the front of their classic log cabin, and as I pull up out front, I note that Kobe's pickup isn't here. I guess I should have called ahead, but I like doing things the old-fashioned way. I grew up in the mountains, and if you wanted to visit your neighbor, and by neighbor I mean any other mountain dweller, you just turned up.

As I cut the engine, I realize there's someone sitting on the front steps.

A woman is hunched over on the stairs that lead down from the front porch. She's clutching something close to her chest, and her brown eyes are wide and staring. She's as frightened as a deer in the forest, and the way she's poised, with a hand on the banister and one foot on the bottom steps, ready to leap up at any moment, she's just as flighty.

We stare at each other, her breathing hard, clearly wondering if she should make a dash for it, and me paralyzed by the vision before me. Because she is a vision. Sunlight dances off her long golden hair as it cascades over her shoulders. She's got pale, smooth skin and full, youthful lips. Hell, she's at least ten years younger than me, but there's something in the set of her eyes, a wariness that makes her look older.

I don't know who she is or why she's here, but

my instinct tells me any sudden movement could scare her off.

Instead of getting out of the car, I wind the window down and we stare at each other. My mouth goes dry as I drink her in. I've never seen anyone so beautiful, and I've got no clue what to say to her.

I clear my throat, and she startles. Christ, the woman's jumpier than a newborn fawn.

"Are you a friend of Hailey's?"

I take a guess that she's here for Kobe's wife. They look about the same age, and I figure if I drop Hailey's name she'll realize I'm not a stranger.

The woman pulls her eyebrows together and adjusts whatever it is she's clutching to her chest.

"Who are you?"

Her voice is bold, and I like that. She may be trembling like a deer, but she's putting on a show of bravado.

"Name's Joseph. I served with Kobe."

She relaxes a little. Being ex-military has that effect on people. They feel they can trust you because you served their country. But the things I saw people doing to each other over there made me lose all hope in humanity. It's why I live deep in the mountains, why I only come out for my motorcycle club or to run errands like this.

The rest of humanity can go to hell. I've seen too

much madness. I've seen what people can do to each other, and I'd rather keep my own company with the animals of the forest.

If it weren't for the Wild Riders MC, I'd never leave my patch of forest at all. I hunt or grow most of the food I need and live off the grid with my own set-up. There's not much I need people for. But Kobe was a brother in arms, and we hunt together sometimes.

"Do you know where Kobe and Hailey are?" the woman asks without telling me her name.

She's afraid of something or someone, I'd bet my best gun on it. A wave of protectiveness hits me so suddenly that I sit back in my seat. I don't know this woman, but I want to keep her safe from whatever she's scared of. I just need her to trust me.

"Dunno. I stopped by to drop some meat off."

Her shoulders sag, and the thing she's holding to her chest moves. She glances down at it and read-justs herself. She's got something alive there, I'm sure. Maybe a puppy or something she found in the woods.

"You been waiting long?"

She stares at me long and hard, and I get the feeling she's assessing me. I tug on my beard, not sure how I measure up. A grizzled mountain man with half a deer in the back of his pickup. If I'd known I was going to meet this beauty today, I would have trimmed my beard and put my best flannel on.

Still, something must work in my favor, because she lets out a long breath and relaxes a little.

"I've been waiting for a few hours."

As she says it, a breeze rustles the surrounding trees, and whatever adrenaline she had warming her veins when I showed up dissipates, because she shivers and hunches over.

As she shivers, the bundle in her arms wriggles again and a thin cry pierces the air. Her attention snaps to the bundle and she bounces it up and down, making shushing noises.

Realization hits me.

"You've got a baby?"

She turns away and pulls the thing closer as if I'm going to jump out and snatch it. My mind's working overtime wondering what the hell this young woman is doing sitting out in the cold with a baby for hours on end in nothing but a thin coat.

I glance around the area in case I've missed something, but there's no sign of a car. No indication of how she got here or what she's doing here. But she's cold and she's got a crying baby. She needs my help.

I open the cab to the pickup and she stands up

and backs onto the deck, the flighty look coming into her eyes.

I hold my hands up.

"I'm not gonna hurt you. The wind's picking up and you look cold."

She bounces the baby and stares at me but doesn't respond. Tiny cries echo around the forest, and the sound is so alien to me it makes me wince. I turn away before she can see and get the blanket from the back.

I want to wrap it around her myself, take care of her so she can take care of her baby. But I sense any movement might scare her take off. And it's important to me that I keep talking to her.

I walk to the bottom of the stairs and hold the blanket up. She snatches it off me and retreats to the deck. Ignoring herself, she wraps it around the child, tucking it around the small body and leaving half of it trailing down her hip.

There's a small backpack leaning against the front door, but she doesn't appear to have anything else with her. I wonder again who she is and what she's doing here and why I feel so damn protective of her.

I can't leave her here on her own, especially with a baby.

"You want to call them and see if you can find out when they're coming home?"

She nods. "My phone's out of battery. I left in a hurry…" She snaps her mouth shut as if she's said too much.

I want to admonish her for venturing into the mountains on her own with only a light jacket and no means of communication. But she's obviously not from around here and doesn't know how dangerous the mountain can be. She probably doesn't even have bear spray.

I slide my phone out of my pocket.

"I don't have Hailey's number, but you can call Kobe."

I hold out the phone, and she takes it with her free arm. I'm rewarded with a small smile.

"Thank you."

I can hear the tone indicating that the call's not connecting. Wherever Kobe is he hasn't got signal, which isn't unusual. Parts of the mountain are blissfully still dark spots.

She hands back the phone, and her eyebrows are knit together with worry. The baby scrunches up its face and lets out a bellow.

"She's hungry."

There's a desperate tone to her voice, and I guess she hasn't got any food with her.

"I've got deer in the back if she wants some?"

It's meant to be a joke, even I know you don't feed raw meat to a baby, but the woman frowns. "She's not on solids yet. I've got milk in my bag but no way to heat it."

She sticks her chin out, daring me to call her a bad mother. Hell, I'm not judging. I don't know her circumstances, but I guess she wouldn't be out here in the cold with an infant if there wasn't a damn good reason for it.

"I can call some people and see if anyone knows where Kobe and Hailey are."

She tugs on her lower lip and looks away. She's worried about something. Maybe she doesn't want anyone to know she's here.

"I'll call Symon, the ranger. He knows the comings and goings of everyone on this mountain, and he's discreet."

She looks back at me and nods.

I bring up Symon's number as she jiggles the baby on her hip.

"Who will I say is looking for them?"

She bits her lip again, leaving imprints from her teeth. She worries it a lot, and I long to run my thumb over the puckered skin and smooth it out.

"Trish," she finally says. "I'm Hailey's sister."

"Trish." I like the sound of her name. It's fierce like she is. "I'll call the ranger."

I make the call to Symon, but no one picks up. I leave him a quick message without mentioning Trish.

Next, I call the Wild Taste Bar and Restaurant. It's where the HQ for the Wild Riders MC is based. Kobe and Hailey often come over for lunch or a drink. Every man in the MC is ex-military, and Kobe knows a fair few of us. He's social for a mountain man and likes to keep in touch, but we all know he's checking in on us. Making sure no one falls over the edge of the precipice that so many of us came back tottering along.

Kendra picks up the phone. She's Barrel's sister and Hops's old lady. That caused a huge stir and nearly got Hops banished from the club, but luckily they sorted out their differences.

"Are Kobe and Hailey up there?"

Kendra checks the restaurant, but no one's seen them. Hops is speaking in the background, and Kendra must hand the phone across to him.

"They're away for the weekend. Went to the coast."

That will explain the phone. They've probably got a remote spot where there's no signal. Having some time together before the baby arrives.

"I went up there to give Kobe some deer meat and found a girl on their doorstep. Says she's Hailey's sister."

Trish gives me a worried look, but I can trust my MC brothers. They won't breathe a word.

"Is she okay?" Kendra asks.

I glance at Trish, and she's cradling the baby. The shushing seems to have worked, but all of a sudden the infant lifts its tiny pink head and gives an almighty wail.

"Is that a baby?" asks Hops.

The pink mouth is contorted into an angry cry that's so loud it's scaring the birds away.

"Yup, she's got a baby with her."

Trish bounces the infant on her shoulder as she paces the porch. Tiny fingers grasp at her hair, and she looks down at the pink scrunched up face with love. Even though the thing is screaming at her, even though it's cold and windy and I just felt the first drops of rain, all I see emanating from her is love.

A bolt of realization shoots through my veins. I want that love trained on me.

The thought is so strong it makes me stagger. I don't know anything about this curvy beauty, but she's vulnerable out here. Her and the baby, they need me. My heart does a little flip, and my chest swells with new purpose.

Whatever this woman is running from, whatever she and her baby need, I will provide. A surge of protectiveness rushes through me, and I know I'll do whatever it takes to keep Trish and her baby safe.

Kendra's saying something on the other end of the line, asking if they need help, but I barely hear her. I know my purpose; I know what I need to do.

"She's fine," I say. "I'll take care of it."

I hang up the phone and slide it back in my pocket. I've never been around a baby, and it's been years since I was with a woman. But I'll do whatever I need to do to take care of these two.

GET YOUR FREE BOOKS

Sign up to the Sadie King mailing list and get access to all the bonus content including bonus scenes and five FREE steamy short romances!

You'll be the first to hear about new releases, exclusive offers, bonus content and all my news. You can even email me back. I love chatting with my readers!

To claim your free books visit:

authorsadieking.com/bonus-scenes

If you're already a subscriber check your last email for the link that will take you straight to the bonus content.

For a full list of Sadie King's books visit her website

www.authorsadieking.com

ABOUT THE AUTHOR

Sadie King is a USA Today Best Selling Author of contemporary romance novellas.

She lives in New Zealand with her ex-military husband and raucous young son.

When she's not writing she loves catching waves with her son, running along the beach, and drinking good wine with a book in hand.

Keep in touch when you sign up for her newsletter. You'll snag yourself a free short romance and access to all the bonus content!

authorsadieking.com/bonus-scenes

Printed in Great Britain
by Amazon